*To Mark and Jamie for believing in
our story and helping us tell it.*

by Julie Verner, PhD

illustrated by Jillian Verner

book design by Amy Wheless

Library of Congress Cataloging-in-Publication Data available.
ISBN: 978-1-949480-01-6

Printed in China

10 9 8 7 6 5 4 3 2 1

Roundtree Press
Petaluma, CA 94952
www.roundtreepress.com

the incredible shrinking girl
a divorce story

by Julie Verner, PhD

illustrated by Jillian Verner

Roundtree Press

Monday morning and no school!

"Woo-hoo!"

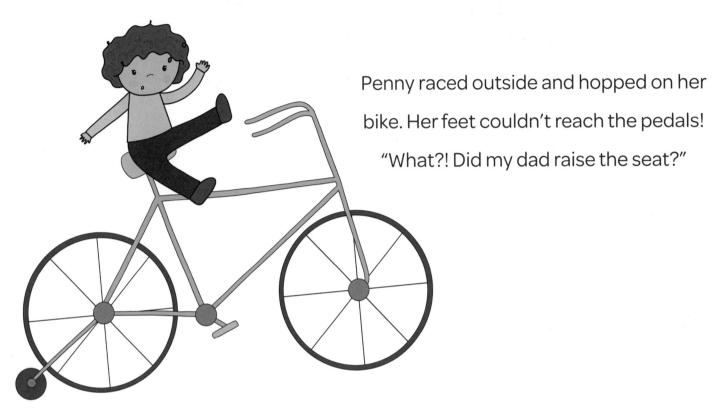

Penny raced outside and hopped on her bike. Her feet couldn't reach the pedals! "What?! Did my dad raise the seat?"

She pulled out her roller skates, but they didn't feel right either. They looked like her skates, but they felt BIG like Daddy's.

Wednesday morning, Penny finished her cereal.

"I'm going to surprise Mommy by rinsing my dish!"

Only she couldn't reach the faucet.

"What the heck?!"

Thursday morning, Penny got dressed for school.

"I've heard of clothes shrinking, but never children!"

"I guess these will have to do."

Ever since Penny learned of her parents'
divorce, she had begun to feel smaller.

She felt small when her dad didn't answer her right away. He seemed like he was lost in space.

She felt teensy-weensy since her mom had become so busy. Penny's parents just seemed so different.

Penny felt
especially
microscopic
when her
parents
fought.

It was like

she

wasn't

even

there.

Friday morning at school, Penny could barely reach her desk.

With a tippy-toe stretch and a great big heave, she jumped into her seat.

Penny did her best to blend in, hoping

nobody would notice just how

tiny she'd become.

The sound of the morning recess bell was followed by Mrs. Bennett's footsteps. "Penny, I noticed that you have been looking a little small lately. Is everything okay?"

Penny froze. Her cheeks and forehead felt warm. She looked down at her tiny feet and then up at Mrs. Bennett's kind and warm eyes.

Before Penny knew it, her words began to tumble out.

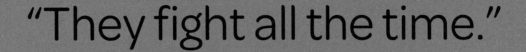

"They fight all the time."

Some of the words surprised Penny like when she heard herself say . . .

"I feel like my parents' divorce is all my fault."

As the story grew, so did Penny.

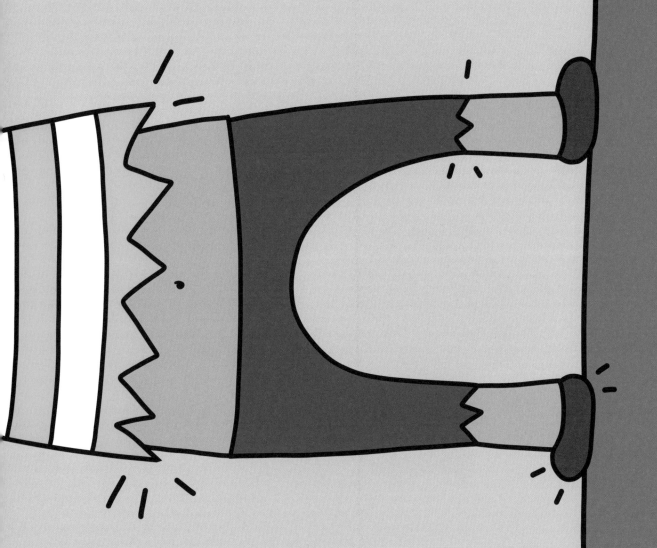

Her pants got tight. Her shoes were too small.

Her voice felt big and strong.

Mrs. Bennet didn't seem surprised. "When I was

nine years old, my parents got a divorce.

I was afraid to tell anyone about my feelings.

I kept it all in and I began to shrink, too.

"I got so small that I had to comb my

hair with my toothbrush!

"One day, my grandmother took me out for a triple scoop of bubblegum ice cream.

"Her eyes were kind and warm, and I couldn't help but share my story. And once I did, I began to grow, too."

Mrs. Bennett explained to Penny, "When your parents decided that they couldn't be married anymore, it was an adult decision with adult reasons. That is their divorce story."

She continued, "But you have a divorce story, too. It's about your thoughts, and feelings, and the changes that happen to you. When you keep your story inside, you start to feel very small. But when you share your story to safe ears and kind eyes, you grow very strong."

Mrs. Bennett handed Penny
a book. The pages were blank,
but the cover wasn't. In Mrs.
Bennett's extra-loopy cursive,
Penny read the words,

Penny's Story.

Penny opened the book to
discover a little poem written
especially for her.

Inside your heart are feelings
that only you can show.
Not right or wrong or good or bad,
just part of what you know.
They tell you what you love,
Whisper what you need.
They like to be respected
And given space to breathe.
Sometimes they speak in giggles,

Or maybe in a tear.
They might come out in a
picture you draw,
Or words you write in here.
I hope you'll share your story,
Feelings, old and new,
Words unique and special,
A tale that's born in you.
Love,
      Mrs. Bennett

And so, Penny kept on sharing and kept on growing.

She believed that her story was unique and special

and THAT made her feel like a very incredible girl!

a note to parents

Going through a big family change such as divorce involves a lot of different feelings for kids and adults. Sometimes, parents' feelings are so big that it makes it difficult for them to understand the needs and experiences of their kids. Children are very sensitive to the feelings of their parents and observe more than their parents realize or like to admit. Children can even feel responsible for the breakdown of the family. They may struggle to share openly and honestly with their parent or caregiver because they don't want to hurt anyone's feelings. Children can find themselves "caught in the middle." One of the best ways you can support your children through the transition of divorce is to provide a safe and neutral place for them to share their story. Teachers, spiritual leaders, therapists, and mentors are just a few examples of people who can help your child. With lots of love and support, even seasons of challenge can become opportunities for growth.

questions to ask

1. Penny was brave when she told her story to Mrs. Bennett. What is the bravest thing you've ever done?

2. Is sharing your divorce story mostly easy or kind of hard?

3. What qualities make someone a good listener?

4. How do you feel when you share about yourself with a good listener?

5. Is there someone new with whom you would like to share your divorce story?